Listen,
My Children

POEMS FOR THIRD GRADERS

A CORE KNOWLEDGE® BOOK

LISTEN, MY CHILDREN: POEMS FOR THIRD GRADERS
ONE IN A SERIES, *POEMS FOR KINDERGARTNERS—FIFTH GRADERS*,
COLLECTING THE POEMS IN THE *CORE KNOWLEDGE SEQUENCE*

A CORE KNOWLEDGE® BOOK

SERIES EDITOR: SUSAN TYLER HITCHCOCK
RESEARCHER: JEANNE NICHOLSON SILER
EDITORIAL ASSISTANT: KRISTEN D. MOSES
CONSULTANT: STEPHEN B. CUSHMAN
GENERAL EDITOR: E. D. HIRSCH JR.

LIBRARY OF CONGRESS CARD CATALOG NUMBER: 00-111615
ISBN 1-890517-31-3

PRINTED IN CANADA
DESIGN BY DIANE NELSON GRAPHIC DESIGN
COVER ART COPYRIGHT © BY LANCE HIDY, LANCE@LANCEHIDY.COM

CORE KNOWLEDGE FOUNDATION
801 EAST HIGH STREET
CHARLOTTESVILLE, VIRGINIA 22902
WWW.COREKNOWLEDGE.ORG

About this Book

"LISTEN, MY CHILDREN, and you shall hear . . ." So begins a famous poem about Paul Revere, written by Henry Wadsworth Longfellow in 1855. This opening line reminds us that every time we read a poem, we hear that poem as well. The sounds and rhythms of the words are part of the poem's meaning. Poems are best understood when read out loud, or when a reader hears the sounds of the words in his or her head while reading silently.

This six-volume series collects all the poems in the Core Knowledge Sequence for kindergarten through fifth grade. Each volume includes occasional notes about the poems and biographical sketches about the poems' authors, but the focus is really the poems themselves. Some have been chosen because they reflect times past; others because of their literary fame; still others were selected because they express states of mind shared by many children.

This selection of poetry, part of the *Core Knowledge Sequence,* is based on the work of E. D. Hirsch Jr., author of *Cultural Literacy* and *The Schools We Need.* The Sequence outlines a core curriculum for preschool through grade eight in English and language arts, history and geography, math, science, art, and music. It is designed to ensure that children are exposed to the essential knowledge that establishes cultural literacy as they also acquire a broad, firm foundation for higher-level schooling. Its first version was developed in 1990 at a convention of teachers and subject matter experts. Revised in 1995 to reflect the classroom experience of Core Knowledge teachers, the Sequence is now used in hundreds of schools across America. Its content also guides the Core Knowledge Series, *What Your Kindergartner—Sixth Grader Needs to Know.*

Contents

Catch a Little Rhyme   7
Eve Merriam

By Myself   8
Eloise Greenfield

Knoxville, Tennessee   9
Nikki Giovanni

Dream Variations   11
Langston Hughes

Adventures of Isabel   12
Ogden Nash

The Crocodile   15
Lewis Carroll

Father William   16
Lewis Carroll

Eletelephony   18
Laura Richards

Jimmy Jet and His TV Set   19
Shel Silverstein

First Thanksgiving of All   20
Nancy Byrd Turner

For want of a nail   21
Author unknown

Trees   23
Joyce Kilmer

—— FOR ADDITIONAL READING ——

Hiawatha's Childhood   24
Henry Wadsworth Longfellow

When Earth Becomes an "It"   29
Marilou Awiakta

Acknowledgments   30

Catch a Little Rhyme

by Eve Merriam

Once upon a time
I caught a little rhyme

I set it on the floor
but it ran right out the door

I chased it on my bicycle
but it melted to an icicle

I scooped it up in my hat
but it turned into a cat

I caught it by the tail
but it stretched into a whale

I followed it in a boat
but it changed into a goat

When I fed it tin and paper
it became a tall skyscraper

Then it grew into a kite
and flew far out of sight . . .

By Myself

by Eloise Greenfield

When I'm by myself
And I close my eyes
I'm a twin
I'm a dimple in a chin
I'm a room full of toys
I'm a squeaky noise
I'm a gospel song
I'm a gong
I'm a leaf turning red
I'm a loaf of brown bread
I'm a whatever I want to be
An anything I care to be
And when I open my eyes
What I care to be
Is me

Knoxville, Tennessee

by Nikki Giovanni

I always like summer
best
you can eat fresh corn
from daddy's garden
and okra
and greens
and cabbage
and lots of
barbecue
and buttermilk
and homemade ice-cream
at the church picnic
and listen to
gospel music
outside
at the church
homecoming
and go to the mountains with
your grandmother
and go barefooted
and be warm
all the time
not only when you go to bed
and sleep

Langston Hughes
1902—1967

Some people call Langston Hughes the "poet
laureate of Harlem," because he wrote so many
poems about life in that neighborhood of New
York City. He started writing during the "Harlem
Renaissance" of the 1920s, when African-American
artists in New York were creating jazz, dance,
theater, and literature together. His home at 20
East 127th Street in Harlem is now a historic
landmark.

Dream Variations

by Langston Hughes

To fling my arms wide
In some place of the sun,
To whirl and to dance
Till the white day is done.
Then rest at cool evening
Beneath a tall tree
While night comes on gently,
    Dark like me —
That is my dream!

To fling my arms wide
In the face of the sun,
Dance! Whirl! Whirl!
Till the quick day is done.
Rest at pale evening . . .
A tall, slim tree . . .
Night coming tenderly
    Black like me.

Adventures of Isabel

by Ogden Nash

Isabel met an enormous bear,
Isabel, Isabel, didn't care;
The bear was hungry, the bear was ravenous,
The bear's big mouth was cruel and cavernous.
The bear said, Isabel, glad to meet you,
How do, Isabel, now I'll eat you!
Isabel, Isabel, didn't worry,
Isabel didn't scream or scurry.
She washed her hands and she straightened her hair up,
Then Isabel quietly ate the bear up.

Once in a night as black as pitch
Isabel met a wicked old witch.
The witch's face was cross and wrinkled,
The witch's gums with teeth were sprinkled.
Ho ho, Isabel! the old witch crowed,
I'll turn you into an ugly toad!
Isabel, Isabel, didn't worry,
Isabel didn't scream or scurry,
She showed no rage and she showed no rancor,
But she turned the witch into milk and drank her.

Isabel met a hideous giant,
Isabel continued self-reliant.
The giant was hairy, the giant was horrid,
He had one eye in the middle of his forehead.
Good morning, Isabel, the giant said,
I'll grind your bones to make my bread.
Isabel, Isabel, didn't worry,
Isabel didn't scream or scurry,
She nibbled the Zwieback that she always fed off,
And when it was gone, she cut the giant's head off.

ZWIEBACK
Hard, sweet, dry toast.

Isabel met a troublesome doctor,
He punched and he poked till he really shocked her.
The doctor's talk was of coughs and chills
And the doctor's satchel bulged with pills.
The doctor said unto Isabel,
Swallow this, it will make you well.
Isabel, Isabel, didn't worry,
Isabel didn't scream or scurry.
She took those pills from the pill concocter,
And Isabel calmly cured the doctor.

CONCOCTER
Someone who concocts, or someone who designs or makes.

Lewis Carroll
1832–1898

Lewis Carroll was another name for Charles Lutwidge Dodgson, a mathematics teacher at Oxford University in England. He didn't want to put his real name on the children's books he wrote: *Alice's Adventures in Wonderland* and *Through the Looking Glass*. Those books began when he was telling stories to three sisters. One of the sisters, named Alice Liddell, liked Mr. Dodgson's stories so much, she asked him to write them down.

This poem comes from *Alice's Adventures in Wonderland*. After falling down the rabbit's hole, Alice wants to be sure she's still herself. As a test, she tries to recite a poem. She probably meant to recite this serious poem written by Isaac Watts, called "Against Idleness and Mischief":

> How doth the little busy bee
>> Improve each shining hour,
> And gather honey all the day,
>> From every opening flower!
>
> How skillfully she builds her cell!
>> How neat she spreads the wax!
> And labours hard to store it well
>> With the sweet food she makes.

When you compare the two poems, you see that Carroll was up to some mischief himself!

The Crocodile

by Lewis Carroll

How doth the little crocodile
    Improve his shining tail,
And pour the waters of the Nile
    On every golden scale!

How cheerfully he seems to grin!
    How neatly spreads his claws,
And welcomes little fishes in
    With gently smiling jaws!

Father William

by Lewis Carroll

"You are old, Father William," the young man said,
"And your hair has become very white;
And yet you incessantly stand on your head—
Do you think, at your age, it is right?"

"In my youth," Father William replied to his son,
"I feared it might injure the brain;
But now that I'm perfectly sure I have none,
Why, I do it again and again."

"You are old," said the youth, "as I mentioned before,
And have grown most uncommonly fat;
Yet you turned a back somersault in at the door—
Pray, what is the reason of that?"

"In my youth," said the sage, as he shook his gray locks,
  "I kept all my limbs very supple
By the use of this ointment — one shilling the box —
  Allow me to sell you a couple?"

"You are old," said the youth, "and your jaws are too weak
  For anything tougher than suet;
Yet you finished the goose, with the bones and the beak—
  Pray how did you manage to do it?"

SUET
Beef fat.

"In my youth," said his father, "I took to the law,
  And argued each case with my wife;
And the muscular strength which it gave to my jaw
  Has lasted the rest of my life."

"You are old," said the youth, "one would hardly suppose
  That your eye was as steady as ever;
Yet you balanced an eel on the end of your nose—
  What made you so awfully clever?"

"I have answered three questions, and that is enough,"
  Said his father. "Don't give yourself airs!
Do you think I can listen all day to such stuff?
  Be off, or I'll kick you downstairs!"

GIVE YOURSELF AIRS
Imagine yourself capable of grand things.

Like "The Crocodile," this poem is recited by Alice while she is in Wonderland. She meets a caterpillar, who tells her it is "wrong from beginning to end," probably because it doesn't match a well-known poem of the time, called "The Old Man's Comforts and How He Gained Them."

Eletelephony

by Laura Richards

Once there was an elephant,
Who tried to use the telephant —
No! No! I mean an elephone
Who tried to use the telephone —
(Dear me! I am not certain quite
That even now I've got it right.)

Howe'er it was, he got his trunk
Entangled in the telephunk;
The more he tried to get it free,
The louder buzzed the telephee —
(I fear I'd better drop the song
Of elephop and telephong!)

Jimmy Jet and His TV Set

by Shel Silverstein

I'll tell you the story of Jimmy Jet —
And you know what I tell you is true.
He loved to watch his TV set
Almost as much as you.

He watched all day, he watched all night
Till he grew pale and lean,
From "The Early Show" to "The Late Late Show"
And all the shows between.

He watched till his eyes were frozen wide,
And his bottom grew into his chair.
And his chin turned into a tuning dial,
And antennae grew out of his hair.

And his brains turned into TV tubes,
And his face to a TV screen.
And two knobs saying "VERT." and "HORIZ."
Grew where his ears had been.

And he grew a plug that looked like a tail
So we plugged in little Jim.
And now instead of him watching TV
We all sit around and watch him.

> When Shel Silverstein was young, televisions were just being developed. They could only show black-and-white pictures, and often those pictures had to be adjusted. Sometimes the picture wiggled side to side, and you adjusted it by turning a knob marked "Vertical." Sometimes the picture rolled up or down, and you adjusted it with a knob marked "Horizontal."

First Thanksgiving of All

by Nancy Byrd Turner

Peace and Mercy and Jonathan,
And Patience (very small),
Stood by the table giving thanks
The first Thanksgiving of all.
There was very little for them to eat,
Nothing special and nothing sweet;
Only bread and a little broth,
And a bit of fruit (and no tablecloth);
But Peace and Mercy and Jonathan
And Patience, in a row,
Stood up and asked a blessing on
Thanksgiving, long ago.
Thankful they were their ship had come
Safely across the sea;
Thankful they were for hearth and home,
And kin and company;
They were glad of broth to go with their bread,
Glad their apples were round and red,
Glad of mayflowers they would bring
Out of the woods again next spring.
So Peace and Mercy and Jonathan,
And Patience (very small),
Stood up gratefully giving thanks
The first Thanksgiving of all.

For want of a nail

Author unknown

For want of a nail, the shoe was lost,
For want of the shoe, the horse was lost,
For want of a horse, the rider was lost,
For want of a rider, the battle was lost,
For want of the battle, the kingdom was lost,
And all for the want of a horseshoe nail.

Joyce Kilmer
1886-1918

Alfred Joyce Kilmer, an American poet and journalist, served as a sergeant in World War I and was killed while fighting in France at the age of 32. Today he is remembered for this famous poem. A forest in North Carolina, one of the few places in the United States where people have never cut down trees, was named after him. The Joyce Kilmer Memorial Forest has trees so large that four people holding hands can't reach all the way around.

Trees

by Joyce Kilmer

I think that I shall never see
A poem lovely as a tree.

A tree whose hungry mouth is pressed
Against the earth's sweet flowing breast;

A tree that looks at God all day,
And lifts her leafy arms to pray;

A tree that may in summer wear
A nest of robins in her hair;

Upon whose bosom snow has lain;
Who intimately lives with rain.

Poems are made by fools like me,
But only God can make a tree.

Hiawatha's Childhood

from The Song of Hiawatha
by Henry Wadsworth Longfellow

By the shores of Gitche Gumee,
By the shining Big-Sea-Water,
Stood the wigwam of Nokomis,
Daughter of the Moon, Nokomis.
Dark behind it rose the forest,
Rose the black and gloomy pine-trees,
Rose the firs with cones upon them;
Bright before it beat the water,
Beat the clear and sunny water,
Beat the shining Big-Sea-Water.

There the wrinkled old Nokomis
Nursed the little Hiawatha,
Rocked him in his linden cradle,
Bedded soft in moss and rushes,
Safely bound with reindeer sinews;
Stilled his fretful wail by saying,
"Hush! the Naked Bear will hear thee!"
Lulled him into slumber, singing,

"Ewa-yea! my little owlet!
Who is this, that lights the wigwam?
With his great eyes lights the wigwam?
Ewa-yea! my little owlet!"

Many things Nokomis taught him
Of the stars that shine in heaven;
Showed him Ishkoodah, the comet,
Ishkoodah, with fiery tresses;
Showed the Death-Dance of the spirits,
Warriors with their plumes and war-clubs,
Flaring far away to northward
In the frosty nights of winter;
Showed the broad white road in heaven,
Pathway of the ghosts, the shadows,
Running straight across the heavens,
Crowded with the ghosts, the shadows.

At the door on summer evenings,
Sat the little Hiawatha;
Heard the whispering of the pine-trees,
Heard the lapping of the waters,
Sounds of music, words of wonder;
"Minne-wawa!" said the pine-trees,
"Mudway-aushka!" said the water.

Saw the fire-fly Wah-wah-taysee,
Flitting through the dusk of evening,
With the twinkle of its candle
Lighting up the brakes and bushes,
And he sang the song of children,
Sang the song Nokomis taught him:

"Wah-wah-taysee, little fire-fly,
Little flitting, white-fire insect,
Little, dancing, white-fire creature,
Light me with your little candle,
Ere upon my bed I lay me,
Ere in sleep I close my eyelids!"

Saw the moon rise from the water,
Rippling, rounding from the water,
Saw the flecks and shadows on it,
Whispered, "What is that, Nokomis?"
And the good Nokomis answered:
"Once a warrior, very angry,
Seized his grandmother, and threw her
Up into the sky at midnight;
Right against the moon he threw her;
'Tis her body that you see there."

Saw the rainbow in the heaven,
In the eastern sky the rainbow,
Whispered, "What is that, Nokomis?"
And the good Nokomis answered:
"'Tis the heaven of flowers you see there;
All the wild-flowers of the forest,
All the lilies of the prairie,
When on earth they fade and perish,
Blossom in that heaven above us."

When he heard the owls at midnight,
Hooting, laughing in the forest,
"What is that?" he cried in terror;

"What is that," he said, "Nokomis?"
And the good Nokomis answered:
"That is but the owl and owlet,
Talking in their native language,
Talking, scolding at each other."

  Then the little Hiawatha
Learned of every bird its language,
Learned their names and all their secrets,
How they built their nests in summer,
Where they hid themselves in winter,
Talked with them whene'er he met them,
Called them "Hiawatha's Chickens."

  Of all beasts he learned the language,
Learned their names and all their secrets,
How the beavers built their lodges,
Where the squirrels hid their acorns,
How the reindeer ran so swiftly,
Why the rabbit was so timid,
Talked with them whene'er he met them,
Called them "Hiawatha's Brothers."

This poem and the next poem are both about Native
American life. "Hiawatha's Childhood" was written in 1855
by Henry Wadsworth Longfellow, who also wrote "Paul
Revere's Ride." It is interesting to compare his ideas about
Native Americans with those in the next poem, written in
1988 by Marilou Awiakta, a Cherokee/Appalachian poet.

When Earth Becomes an "It"

by Marilou Awiakta

When the people call Earth "Mother,"
they take with love
and with love give back
so that all may live.

When the people call Earth "it,"
they use her
consume her strength.
Then the people die.

Already the sun is hot
out of season.
Our mother's breast
is going dry.
She is taking all green
into her heart
and will not turn back
until we call her
by her name.

Acknowledgments

Every care has been taken to trace and acknowledge copyright of the poems and images in this volume. If accidental infringement has occurred, the editor offers apologies and welcomes communications that allow proper acknowledgment in subsequent editions.

· **"Catch a Little Rhyme"** from *Catch a Little Rhyme* by Eve Merriam. Copyright © 1966 by Eve Merriam, copyright © renewed 1966 by Dee Michael and Guy Michel. Used by permission of Marian Reiner.

"By Myself" from *Honey, I Love* by Eloise Greenfield, text copyright © 1978 by Eloise Greenfield. Used by permission of HarperCollins Publishers.

"Knoxville, Tennessee" from *Black Feeling, Black Talk, Black Judgment* by Nikki Giovanni. Copyright © 1968, 1970 by Nikki Giovanni. Reprinted with permission of HarperCollins Publishers, Inc.

"Dream Variations" from *Collected Poems* by Langston Hughes. Copyright © 1994 by the Estate of Langston Hughes. Reprinted by permission of Alfred A. Knopf, a Division of Random House, Inc. and by Harold Ober Associates Incorporated.

"Adventures of Isabel" from *The Bad Parents' Garden of Verses* by Ogden Nash. Copyright © 1936 by Ogden Nash, renewed. Reprinted by permission of Curtis Brown, Ltd.

"Jimmy Jet and His TV Set" from *Where the Sidewalk Ends* by Shel Silverstein. Copyright © 1974 by Evil Eye Music, Inc. Selection reprinted by permission of HarperCollins Publishers.

"When Earth Becomes an 'It'" from *Selu, Seeking the Corn-Mother's Wisdom* by Marilou Awiakta. Copyright © 1993. Reprinted with permission from Fulcrum Publishing, Inc., Golden, Colorado, USA. All rights reserved.

Images:
Langston Hughes: © CORBIS
Lewis Carroll: © Bettmann/CORBIS